TOP 10

CUTEST
ANIMALS

Children's Press®
An imprint of Scholastic Inc.

BY BRENNA MALONEY

A special thank-you to the team at the Cincinnati Zoo & Botanical Garden for their expert consultation.

Library of Congress Cataloging-in-Publication Data available

ISBN 978-1-5461-3611-8 (library binding)
ISBN 978-1-5461-3612-5 (paperback)

10 9 8 7 6 5 4 3 2 1   25 26 27 28 29

Printed in China   62
First edition, 2025

Book design by Kay Petronio

Photos ©: cover, 1: serikbaib/Getty Images; 4 left: Supakrit Tirayasupasin/Getty Images; 4 top right: nikpal/Getty Images; 4 center right: Steven Tessy/Getty Images; 5 top left: CB2/ZOB/Supplied by WENN.com/Newscom; 5 top right: Hiroki Takahashi/Solent News/Shutterstock; 5 bottom right: Temujin Nana/Getty Images; 6 main: praisaeng/Getty Images; 6 pineapple: Valengilda/Getty Images; 10–11 main: Dzulfikri Dzulfikri/500px/Getty Images; 10 spatula: Veni vidi...shoot/Getty Images; 11 bottom right: YinYang/Getty Images; 12–13 main: Piotr Naskrecki/Minden Pictures; 13 bottom right: André Gilden/Getty Images; 16–17 main: Jeff Mauritzen/Design Pics Inc/Alamy Images; 16 bottom: bonetta/Getty Images; 17 inset: Ben Cranke/Getty Images; 18–19 main: CB2/ZOB/Supplied by WENN.com/Newscom; 19 bottom right: Joyce Gross; 20–21 main: Tyrone Ping/iNaturalist; 22 orange: Tuomas A. Lehtinen/Getty Images; 24–25 main: Matthias Haker Photography/Getty Images; 26 main: Gerald Corsi/Getty Images; 26 child: baona/Getty Images; 27: Temujin Nana/Getty Images; 28–29 main: Gerald Corsi/Getty Images; 28 inset: David McGowen/Getty Images; 30 top left: praisaeng/Getty Images; 30 top right: Gerald Corsi/Getty Images; 30 bottom center: kata716/Getty Images. All other photos © Shutterstock.

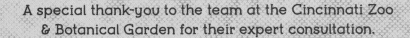

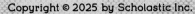

HEDGEHOG

SEA OTTER

CONTENTS

THE WORLD OF CUTE

HONDURAN WHITE BAT

MADAGASCAR DAY GECKO

HEDGEHOG

PIKA

There are so many cute animals in our wild world! Some are fuzzy, furry, or fluffy. Some are sweet or silly. And some are cuddly or colorful.

But . . . are you ready to discover which one is the absolute cutest? Read on and count down from ten to one to learn which animal takes the top spot!

VENEZUELAN POODLE MOTH

ADÉLIE PENGUIN

SHIMA-ENAGA

EMPEROR TAMARIN

SEA OTTER

DESERT RAIN FROG

#10 PRICKLY! HEDGEHOG

FACT FILE

ANIMAL GROUP: Mammal

HABITATS: Woodlands, farmlands, gardens

AVERAGE SIZE: A pineapple

DIET: Omnivore

You can look, but do not touch this prickly cutie! A hedgehog is covered in spines. It searches through hedges to hunt for insects.

You might not see it, but you can hear it. This roly-poly mammal grunts like a pig as it searches. That is why it is called a *hedgehog*. When it gets tired, it tucks its head in toward its belly. It curls its body up into a tight, spiky ball. Nighty night!

FACT

A hog is another name for a pig.

HEDGEHOG CLOSE-UP

SPINES

Stiff, sharp spines are made up of keratin. This is the same material as human hair and nails.

TAIL

A short tail is usually hidden beneath the spines.

LEGS

A hedgehog's legs are about 4 inches (10 cm) long.

An adult hedgehog has between 5,000 and 7,000 spines on its body.

EARS
A hedgehog uses its sense of hearing to search for prey.

FUR
Its face, belly, and legs are covered with soft fur.

EYES
Its eyesight is poor.

FEET
Each foot has five toes. The toes have sharp claws to run, dig, and climb.

MADAGASCAR DAY GECKO

COLORFUL!

FACT FILE

ANIMAL GROUP: Reptile

HABITAT: Tropical rainforests

AVERAGE SIZE: A spatula

DIET: Carnivore

This cute little reptile seems to have a smile on its face! The Madagascar day gecko has a bright green body. Unlike other geckos, this one is active during the day.

This gecko scampers up and down trees. Its red lines and spots help it blend in, or **camouflage**. It can hide among leaves and colorful flowers. It also lies in the sun and munches on insects.

FACT This gecko even has a cute voice! It can squeak, click, bark, and croak.

TINY!

HONDURAN WHITE BAT

ANIMAL GROUP: Mammal

HABITAT: Rainforests

AVERAGE SIZE:
A golf tee

DIET: Frugivore

Have you ever seen a tiny white bat? Its ears, nose, and lips are bright yellow. This cutie uses the edges of leaves to make a tent.

The leaf tent protects the bat from rain, the hot sun, and **predators**. During the day, you will find it snuggled up with other bats. At night, it zips through the air in search of its favorite figs to eat.

#7
PIKA
NIBBLER!

FACT FILE

ANIMAL GROUP: Mammal

HABITAT: Rocky mountains

AVERAGE SIZE: A banana

DIET: Herbivore

This cuddly little mammal has an egg-shaped body. It has rounded ears. A pika spends its day collecting food and eating. It feeds on grass, weeds, and wildflowers.

These plants grow in its rocky, high-mountain habitat. You will probably hear a pika before you see it. Its call is like the bleat of a lamb. When you see one, it will probably have its mouth full!

FACT

Pikas were the inspiration for the Pokémon character Pikachu.

#6
ADÉLIE PENGUIN

SILLY!

This cute little bird is dressed up to party! An Adélie penguin has a black-and-white body. It looks like it is wearing a tuxedo.

The Adélie penguin was named after an explorer's wife, who was named Adéle.

Its body is also built for speed. On land, it might look silly waddling along. But it can slide on its belly over the ice. And in the water . . . watch out! This penguin can reach speeds of up to 9 miles per hour (14 kph)! That is faster than the average running speed for a person. The Adélie penguin uses its speed when hunting. It chases krill, small fish, and squid.

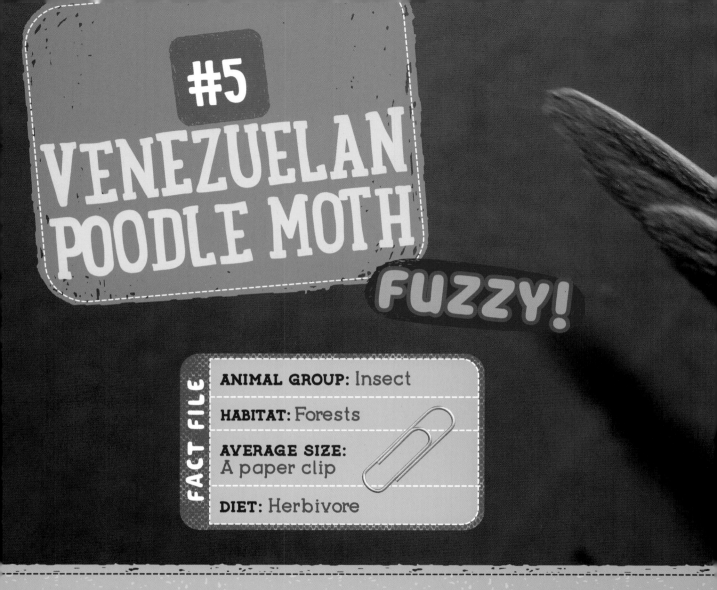

#5

VENEZUELAN POODLE MOTH

FUZZY!

FACT FILE

ANIMAL GROUP: Insect

HABITAT: Forests

AVERAGE SIZE: A paper clip

DIET: Herbivore

This fluffy moth looks more like a poodle! The adorable Venezuelan poodle moth is a mystery. It was discovered in 2009 and not much is known about it.

Its body is covered in fur. Scientists think that its fur **absorbs** sound. If true, that makes it harder for predators like bats to find it. Bats use sound to hunt prey.

This insect has brown antennae that look like long eyelashes!

SQUEAKY!

DESERT RAIN FROG

FACT FILE

ANIMAL GROUP: Amphibian

HABITAT: Sandy shores

AVERAGE SIZE: A walnut

DIET: Insectivore

There are many reasons why this frog is cute! First, it's tiny. Second, it's round, like a ball. Third, it has big eyes. And fourth, it squeaks! It sounds like a dog's chew toy.

The squeaky sound scares away predators. The desert rain frog cannot hop, but it can dig quickly. If it needs to disappear, it hides under the sand.

FACT This frog gets most of the water it needs not from rain but from fog.

#3 SHIMA-ENAGA

FLUFFY!

FACT FILE

ANIMAL GROUP: Bird

HABITAT: Forests

AVERAGE SIZE: A grapefruit

DIET: Omnivore

The shima-enaga looks like a flying cotton ball! In the center of the ball are two shiny black eyes. It has a little black beak. This bird lives in cold **climates**.

To keep warm, it puffs up its fluffy white feathers. The shima-enaga is fast! It flits from tree to tree. It hunts for bugs and seeds to snack on.

FACT These birds are sometimes called snow fairies.

MUSTACHES!

EMPEROR TAMARIN

FACT FILE

ANIMAL GROUP: Mammal

HABITAT: Tropical rainforests

AVERAGE SIZE: A bread knife

DIET: Omnivore

The emperor tamarin is a small monkey. It has a cute mustache. The males have mustaches. The females have mustaches. Even the young have mustaches.

Scientists think their mustaches are how emperor tamarins identify one another. This monkey spends most of its time in trees. It mostly feeds on fruit and insects. It is very playful and highly social.

FACT

The emperor tamarin was named after a German leader with a mustache! His name was Emperor Wilhelm II.

#1 SEA OTTER

FURRY!

FACT FILE

ANIMAL GROUP: Mammal

HABITAT: Oceans

AVERAGE SIZE: A 7-year-old child

DIET: Carnivore

You will find the cutest animal in the ocean! A sea otter looks super cute. It also does cute things. This furry otter likes to sleep on its back while floating.

To keep itself from floating away, it holds paws with another otter. A group of resting otters is called a raft. For meals, a sea otter eats sea urchins, crabs, mussels, and clams. These must all be cracked open. This cutie balances a rock on its belly. It smacks the food against the rock until the shell opens. Dinnertime!

FACT Scientists have seen more than 1,000 sea otters in one raft.

NOSTRILS AND EARS

Both nostrils and ears close when an otter dives.

WHISKERS

Sensitive whiskers help an otter find prey.

TEETH

Otters have strong teeth and a powerful bite.

PAWS

Strong front paws help an otter grip, twist, dig, and pull things apart.

FEET

An otter's back feet are webbed. They look like flippers for swimming.

A sea otter can hold its breath underwater for five minutes.

FACT

FUR
An otter has the thickest fur of any animal!

TAIL
A long, muscular tail helps an otter swim.

SIZING THEM UP

There are so many cute animals in our wild world! Some are cuddly. Some are soft. Some make funny sounds or do silly things. Do you agree the sea otter is the cutest? Or would you pick a different animal? You can probably find even more cute animals and make your own list!

GLOSSARY

absorb (ab-ZORB) to take in something, such as water, in a natural or gradual way

amphibian (am-FIB-ee-uhn) a cold-blooded animal with a backbone that lives in water and breathes with gills when young

camouflage (KAM-uh-flahzh) a disguise or natural coloring that allows animals to hide

carnivore (KAHR-nuh-vor) an animal that eats meat

climate (KLYE-mit) the weather typical of a place over a long period of time

frugivore (FROO-juh-vor) an animal that mostly eats fruit

herbivore (HUR-buh-vor) an animal that only eats plants

insectivore (in-SEK-tuh-vor) an animal that eats insects

keratin (KER-uh-tin) what nails and hair are made of

mammal (MAM-uhl) a warm-blooded animal that has hair or fur and usually gives birth to live babies

omnivore (AHM-nuh-vor) an animal that eats both plants and meat

predator (PRED-uh-tur) an animal that lives by hunting other animals for food

prey (pray) an animal that is hunted by another animal for food

reptile (REP-tile) a cold-blooded animal that crawls across the ground or creeps on short legs; most have backbones and reproduce by laying eggs

INDEX

ABOUT THE AUTHOR

Brenna Maloney is the author of many books. She lives in Washington, DC, with her husband and two sons. She thinks all animals are cute.